PRINCESS MINNA

THE ENCHANTED FOREST

More **ROYALLY EXCITING ADVENTURES** to
look out for:

THE UNICORN MIX-UP

THE BIG BAD SNOWY DAY

THE BEST PRINCESS

written by
KIRSTY APPLEBAUM

illustrated by
SAHAR HAGHGOO

PRINCESS MINNA

THE ENCHANTED FOREST

nosy crow

First published in the UK in 2022 by Nosy Crow Ltd
The Crow's Nest, 14 Baden Place,
Crosby Row, London, SE1 1YW, UK

Nosy Crow Eireann Ltd
44 Orchard Grove, Kenmare,
Co Kerry, V93 FY22, Ireland

Nosy Crow and associated logos are trademarks and/or registered
trademarks of Nosy Crow Ltd.

Text copyright © Kirsty Applebaum, 2022
Cover and inside illustrations copyright © Sahar Haghgoo, 2022

The right of Kirsty Applebaum and Sahar Haghgoo to be identified
as the author and illustrator respectively of this work has been asserted
by them in accordance with the Copyright, Designs
and Patents Act 1988.

ISBN: 978 1 78800 953 9

A CIP catalogue record for this book will be available from the British Library.

Printed and bound in China.

Papers used by Nosy Crow are made from wood grown in sustainable forests.

1 3 5 7 9 10 8 6 4 2

www.nosycrow.com

FOR VICTOR
K. A.

Chapter One

This is Minna. She is a **princess**.
Princess Minna is very good at
lots of things.
She is good at taming unicorns,
kissing frogs and fighting dragons.

Princess Minna lives in

Castle Tall-Towers

with the King, the Queen and a wizard called Raymond. Castle Tall-Towers has some

very

tall towers.

They reach right

up

to the sky. On cloudy days you can't even see the tops of them.

When all is well in the kingdom, lots of grey doves **sweep** and **swoop** around the towers making soft cooing noises. They make the whole castle smell like tutti-frutti ice cream.

When all is **not** well in
the kingdom, big seagulls
fly up from the coast
and scare the doves
away. Then they **flip**
and **flap** around the
towers, making screechy
squawking noises. They
make the whole castle
smell like old seaweed.

One afternoon Princess Minna
was in her bedroom when she
noticed a funny smell.
She sniffed a

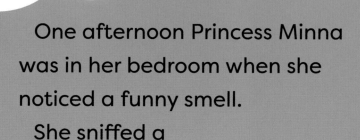

big sniff.

She knew that smell.
She'd sniffed it before.
Seaweed.

Princess Minna looked out of her
window. There were big seagulls
screeching and squawking. The
doves were nowhere to be seen.

Oh dear, she thought.

All is not well.

All is not well at all.

Princess Minna's room was right
at the top of this tower here.

She ran **down**
and **down**
and **down**

and **down**
and **down**
and **down**
until **finally**
she reached
the bottom.

"Oh, Minna!" said the Queen, pulling seagull feathers out of her crown. "**All is not well!**"

"Something **dreadful** has happened," said the King, wiping seagull poo from his velvet robes. "We've just had a phone call from Lord and Lady Welling Tunboot."

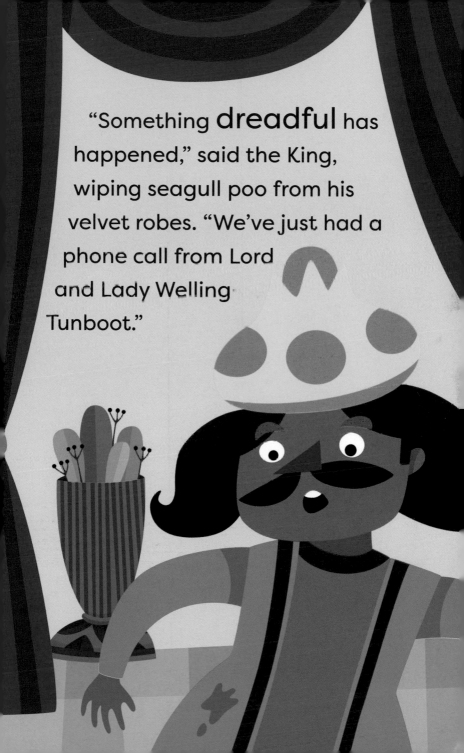

"It's their son's birthday," said Raymond,

magically.

"Yes," said the Queen. "He turns ten years old today."

Prince Welling-Tunboot's birthday? That didn't sound **too** bad, thought Princess Minna. Birthdays were usually quite nice.

"**However**," added the King, "on the day he was born, a

bad fairy

put a **curse** upon him.

She said that
on his tenth
birthday he
would prick
his finger on
the spindle
of a spinning
wheel and fall
asleep ...

13

"... along with everyone else who happened to be near him at the time. Then **thorny bushes** would grow up around the palace, and **fearsome guards** would appear, and if the prince wasn't awoken by sundown he would

never wake again!"

Gosh, thought Princess Minna. "So," said the Queen, "Lord and Lady Welling-Tunboot swore that, on the eve of their son's tenth birthday, they would remove all the spinning wheels from the palace. Then it would be **impossible** for the prince to prick his finger."

"... because **fearsome guards** have appeared and **thorny bushes** have grown up around the palace and the prince and his nanny and the cook and the gardener and the lady who came to deliver the **raspberry-ripple-flavour birthday cake** are all fast asleep and not answering their phones!"

Fearsome guards?
Thorny bushes? Sleeping
prince? **Excellent**, thought
Princess Minna.
"It's a **disaster**," said the King.
"Please go and sort it out, Minna.
Straightaway!"

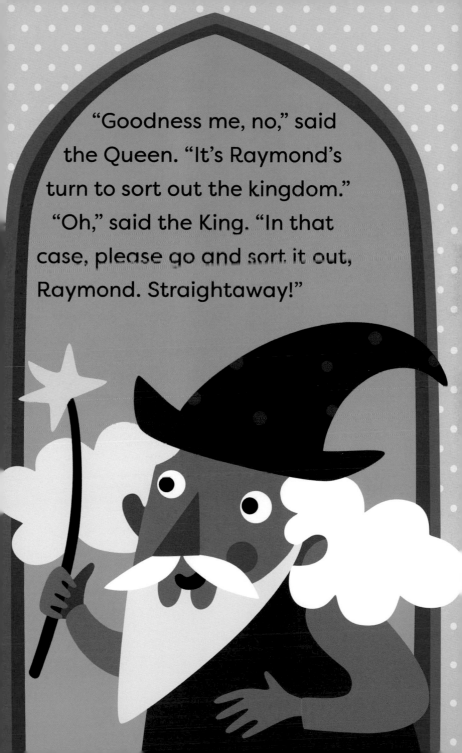

"Goodness me, no," said the Queen. "It's Raymond's turn to sort out the kingdom." "Oh," said the King. "In that case, please go and sort it out, Raymond. Straightaway!"

Raymond flicked through his

**Very Big Book
Of Highly
Magical Spells.**

"Unfortunately," he said,
"I don't have any spells
that will lift a **curse**
cast by a

bad fairy.

Not a single one."

"No matter," cried Princess Minna, already running for the door. "I'll do it!"

Princess Minna **loved** sorting out the kingdom.

"Remember," called the King, "you must reach the prince before sundown, or he will **never wake again**."

"And then where will we be?" called the Queen.

Chapter Two

Tunboot Palace was right in the middle of the **Enchanted Forest** and Princess Minna knew how to get there fast. "**Lorenzo!**" she shouted. "**Lorenzo!**"

Within moments, Lorenzo the dragon had landed in front of the castle. Princess Minna was **very** good at fighting dragons but she never needed to fight Lorenzo. He was her **best friend in the whole world.** She climbed on to his back.

Lorenzo **swung** and **swished** his wings.

Wallooop

wallooop
wallooop!

And they were on their way.

As they **walloooped** through the air, Princess Minna heard an

"Ow!"

She looked down. There on the ground was a swan who looked **very unhappy.**

"Ow! Ow! Ow!"

The swan had one webbed foot curled up underneath her. She cried every time she hopped.

"Lorenzo," said Princess Minna. "We must stop and help that poor swan."

"But Princess Minna," said Lorenzo, "it's quite late and the sun has already started going down. If we stop now you might not have time to awaken the prince.

And also, swans can be quite **dangerous**, you know. My mum always says **never go near a swan, Lorenzo.** They might look lovely but if you give them half a chance they'll break your arm."

33

"That's **nonsense**," said Princess Minna. "We have to go and help her. She's in pain. And anyway, we've got plenty of time. It's just a few guards to fight and some thorny bushes to get past. **Easy-peasy**."

Lorenzo sighed a fiery sigh, then swept down and landed quite close to the swan (but not **too** close).

35

"Oh, Princess Minna!" cried the swan. "I have a drawing pin stuck in my foot. It hurts so much. Will you help me?"

"Of course," said Princess Minna. She knelt down and removed the drawing pin from the swan's foot.

36

"Oh, thank you," said the swan. "How can I **ever** repay you?"

"**No need!**" said Princess Minna. "**No time!** I have to get to the Enchanted Forest before sundown."

"**Oooh** – I like the Enchanted Forest. Can I come too?" said the swan.

"Of course!" said Princess Minna.

So, because the swan seemed quite friendly after all, Lorenzo allowed her to climb on to his back and off they all flew towards the Enchanted Forest.

Wallooop
wallooop
wallooop.

Chapter Three

As they **walloooped** through the air, Princess Minna heard a sob. She looked down. There on the ground was an old lady who looked **very unhappy**.

The old lady had dropped her bag and all her shopping had fallen out.

"Lorenzo," said Princess Minna. "We must **stop** and help that poor old lady."

"But Princess Minna," said Lorenzo, "the sun is halfway down in the sky. If we stop again you might not have time to awaken the prince. And also, old ladies can be quite **dangerous,** you know.

My mum always tells me to stay away from old ladies. They keep **strange magic potions** in their handbags."

"That's nonsense," said Princess Minna. "She's just a harmless little old lady. And as long as we go straight to the **Enchanted Forest** afterwards I can still save the prince. Please, Lorenzo, we must go and help her."

Lorenzo sighed a fiery sigh, then swept down and landed close to the old lady (but not **too** close). "Oh, Princess Minna," sobbed the old lady. "My back hurts so much I can't bend over to pick up all these things. Will you help me?"

"Of course," said Princess Minna. She gathered up the old lady's shopping and packed it back into the bag.

"Oh, thank you," said the old lady. "How can I ever repay you?"

"No need!" said Princess Minna. "No time! I have to get to the Enchanted Forest before sundown."

"Oooh – I like the Enchanted Forest. Can I come too?" said the old lady.

"Of course!" said Princess Minna. So, because the old lady seemed quite friendly after all, Lorenzo allowed her to climb on to his back and off they all flew towards the Enchanted Forest.

Wallooop
wallooop
wallooop.

47

Chapter Four

As they **wallooooped** through the air, Princess Minna heard a "**Baaaaa!**" She looked down. There on the ground was a sheep who looked **very woolly** and **very unhappy**.

The sheep's coat had grown so big that her legs didn't reach the ground anymore.

"Lorenzo," said Princess Minna. "We must stop and help that poor creature."

"But Princess Minna," said Lorenzo, "look at where the sun is! We're going to run out of time and the prince will **never wake up.** The doves will **never come back** to Castle Tall-Towers and the Queen will **always** have seagull feathers in her crown and the King will **always** have seagull poo on his robes.

My mum does like sheep, though. She keeps little sheep ornaments on her windowsill."

"Then your mum would be very unhappy if we didn't stop to help," said Princess Minna. "Please, Lorenzo. I'm **sure** there'll still be time to save the prince."

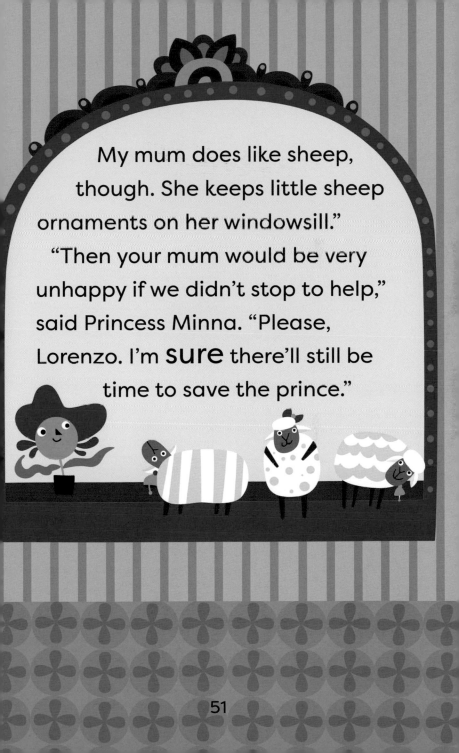

Lorenzo sighed another fiery sigh.
"You are very kind, Princess Minna.
That is why

I love you.

But please be quick." He swept
down and landed next to the
very woolly sheep.

"Baaaa," said the sheep. "No one has sheared me in years and years. Now I'm **SO** woolly that I have to

roll

instead of walk. Princess Minna, will you help me? There's a pair of shears over there."

The sheep waved her front legs towards something that looked like an

enormous

pair of scissors.

"Of course," said Princess Minna. She picked up the

enormous

pair of scissors and began to cut the sheep's coat.

Goodness me, thought Princess Minna. This sheep shearing is very hard work.

A quarter of the way through she had to stop to wipe her **royal brow**. **"Hurry up!"** said the swan.

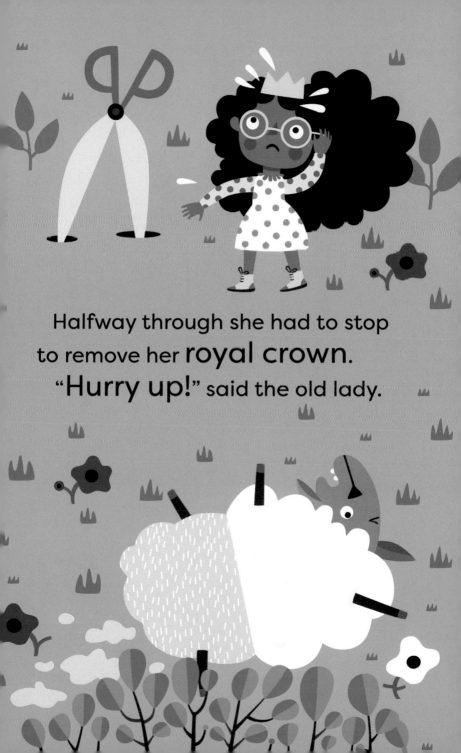

Halfway through she had to stop
to remove her **royal crown.**
"Hurry up!" said the old lady.

Three quarters of the way through she had to stop for a **royal drink.**

"Stop stopping!" said Lorenzo. "We don't have time!"

Eventually Princess Minna
finished shearing the sheep. She
was **very** tired.

"Baaaaaaaa!" The sheep
galloped around. "Oh, Princess
Minna, how can I **ever** repay
you?"

"**No need!**" said Lorenzo.
"**No time!** We must get to the
Enchanted Forest before sundown."

"Oooh – I like the Enchanted Forest. Can I come too?" said the sheep.

So everyone helped the **very tired** Princess Minna on to Lorenzo's back and off they all flew towards the Enchanted Forest.

Wallooop

wallooop
wallooop.

Chapter
Five

Lorenzo landed in the middle of the forest. It was **beautiful**. Enchanted birds sang enchanted songs. Enchanted rabbits played happily alongside enchanted foxes.

But by now the sun was
SO low it nearly touched
the tops of the trees.

63

"Thank goodness you're here, Princess Minna," said Lady Welling-Tunboot. "There's not a moment to spare."

"First, you must get past the **fearsome guards**," said Lord Welling-Tunboot.

He pointed at a row of
**growling, spitting,
snorting**
guards.

Princess Minna was **very** tired
indeed. She stumbled forwards
and yawned a yawn

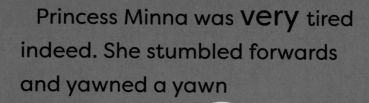

so huge

it made her fall over.
The **fearsome guards**
laughed and laughed. "You'll never
get past us, Princess Minna," they
boomed.

They're right, thought Princess Minna. I'm **much** too late and **much** too tired. And it's

all

my own fault.

She sat on the forest floor and blinked her teary eyes.

The sun began to slip down behind the enchanted trees.

Suddenly a shadow swept overhead.

It was the swan! She swooped at the fearsome guards.

"If you don't let Princess Minna through," she screeched, "I'll break your arms!"

The fearsome guards ducked and screamed and ran for their lives.

"Oh, thank you, Swan!" said Princess Minna.

"You're very welcome," said the swan. "But hurry, you're running out of time."

"Next you must hack through the **thorny bushes**," said Lady Welling-Tunboot.

Lord Welling-Tunboot pointed at a **huge**, dark thicket.

He handed Princess Minna an axe, but she was **SO** tired she couldn't lift it.

"It's no good," she said. "I can't do it.

I'm not going to
be able to save the
prince." She looked up
to the treetops. Only
the very tip of the
sun could be seen
above them.
Night-time
was **almost**
here.

"Don't give up, Princess Minna!"

It was the old lady! She took an **enormous sparkly bottle** out of her bag.

"I just so happen to have a **strange magic potion** that kills thorny bushes but is completely harmless for all other living creatures."

She shook the **strange magic potion** all over the bushes. In seconds they shrivelled up and died.

"Oh, thank you, Old Lady!" said Princess Minna.

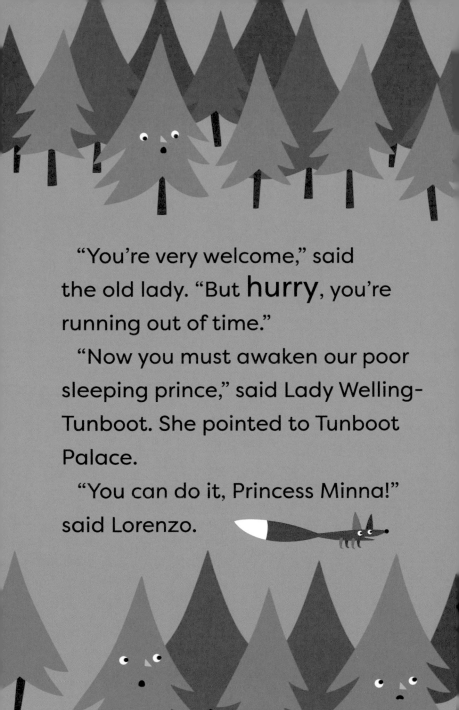

"You're very welcome," said the old lady. "But **hurry**, you're running out of time."

"Now you must awaken our poor sleeping prince," said Lady Welling-Tunboot. She pointed to Tunboot Palace.

"You can do it, Princess Minna!" said Lorenzo.

The sun was nothing but a warm glow above the trees now. But perhaps Lorenzo was right. Perhaps Princess Minna **could** still save the prince.

She decided to pretend she
wasn't tired at all.

She **ran** towards the palace.

"How do I awaken the prince?"
she called over her shoulder.

"With a kiss!"

shouted Lord and Lady Welling-
Tunboot.

"It has to be a kiss!"

A **kiss?**

She had to **kiss** the prince?

Ugh.

Princess Minna didn't mind kissing **frogs.** She was used to that.

But princes?

Ugh.

Still, she was determined to awaken the sleeping boy.

She ran into the palace and
up the stairs ... and there was
Prince Welling-Tunboot, snoring
very loudly.

Snore ... snore.

Just imagine he's a frog, Princess Minna told herself.

Snore ... snore.

She bent forwards, puckered her lips and—

"**Baaaaa!** I'll help you,
Princess Minna!"

The not-very-woolly sheep
galloped in, shoved
Princess Minna out of
the way and gave
the prince a big,
not-very-woolly
kiss right on
the cheek.

The prince awoke, just as the sun disappeared completely and darkness fell over the forest.

Everyone else in the palace woke up too. They all rubbed their sleepy eyes.

"Oh, thank you, Sheep," cried
Princess Minna.

"Baaaaaa," said the sheep.

"Hurrah!" cried Lorenzo
and the old lady and the swan.

"Hurrah!" cried
Lord and Lady
Welling-Tunboot.

"What's going on?" said the prince and his nanny and the cook and the gardener and the lady who'd come to deliver the **raspberry-ripple-flavour birthday cake.**

85

Back at

Castle Tall-Towers

the doves were making soft cooing noises and **everything** smelled like **tutti-frutti** ice cream again. The seagulls were nowhere to be seen.

"Thank goodness,"
said the King,
hoovering up
the last of
the seagull
feathers.

"Thank goodness indeed," agreed the Queen.

Princess Minna
got straight into
bed and fell fast
asleep.
And **all was
well** in the
kingdom once more.